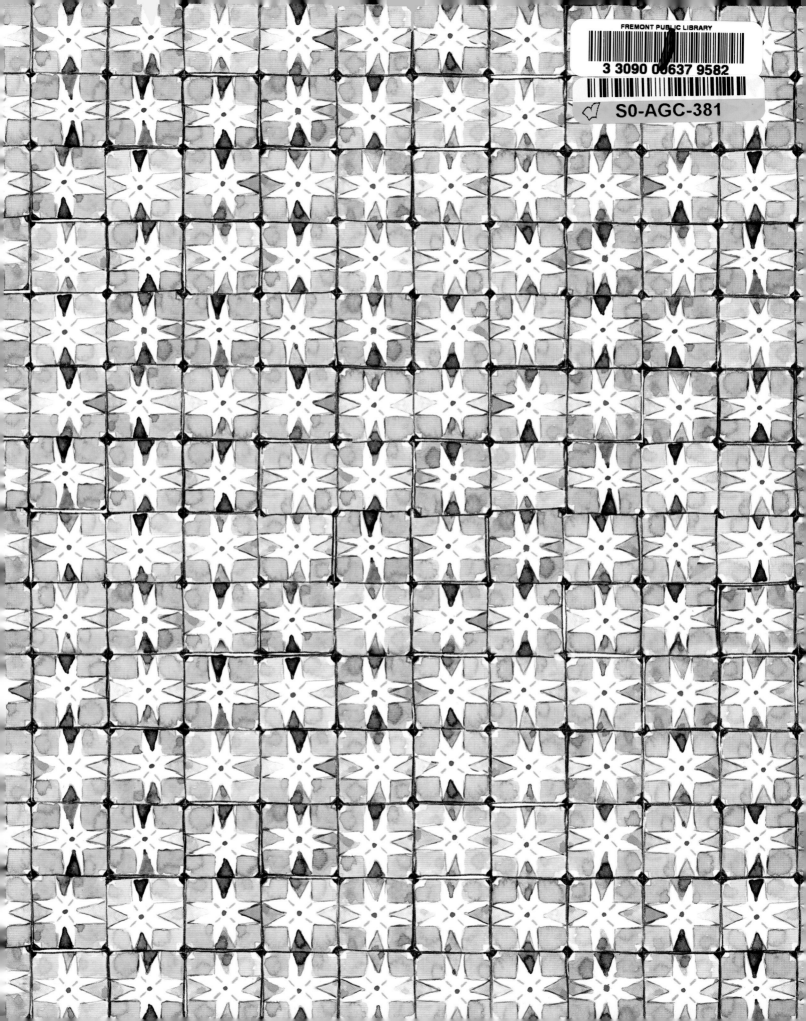

THE CHICKENTOWN mystery

Text and illustrations: Albert Arrayás
Translation: Carine Laforest

CRACKBOOM!

Not far from here, there is a village called Chickentown.

Chickentown is an amazing place. Hens and people live side by side there. Every hen sleeps in a cozy bed and watches TV in a comfortable armchair. Hens even have their own bathrobes.

Hens are beloved members of every family.

Chickentown is also famous for hosting the annual Golden Feather competition, where the Best Hen of the Year is crowned. As you can imagine, winning this competition is just about the most exciting thing that can happen to a hen.

Pearl S. Cluck

Priscilla Callas

Ava Swanneck

Nigella "Minnie" Cooper

Aurora Fairytail

Victoria Peckham

Serena Ruffles

Annie Yolkley

Esther Willyard

Rosie Van der Beak

Coco Azure

Early one morning, a few days before the competition, a frightening cry awakens all the townsfolk. Scarlett, Mrs. Sillyfeather's hen, has disappeared! Strange footprints cover the floor of her room. Who could they belong to?

The following night, another horrible cry disturbs the villagers' sleep. Gwendolyn, the Fairbeak family's hen, has disappeared! There is another clue: Someone has marked the wing chair in her bedroom with sharp claws. Who could they belong to?

By morning, fear grips all of Chickentown.
Mayor Cockscomb sends out citizens' patrols.

But later that night, a terrifying cry pierces the air, rousing everyone from sleep. Rufina, the Cluckaday family's hen, has disappeared! There is a new and bizarre clue: A trail of reddish fur leads out of her bedroom window. Who could it belong to?

Nobody can make any sense of these eerie disappearances.

The following night, Clarabelle, the Spatchcock family's hen, vanishes without a trace! An eyewitness reports seeing a strange shadow moving across her room. Who could it belong to?

This mystery is truly confounding. Fortunately, Chickentown,
like any village worth its salt, has a resident witch.
She is very wise, and her name is Miss Henrietta.

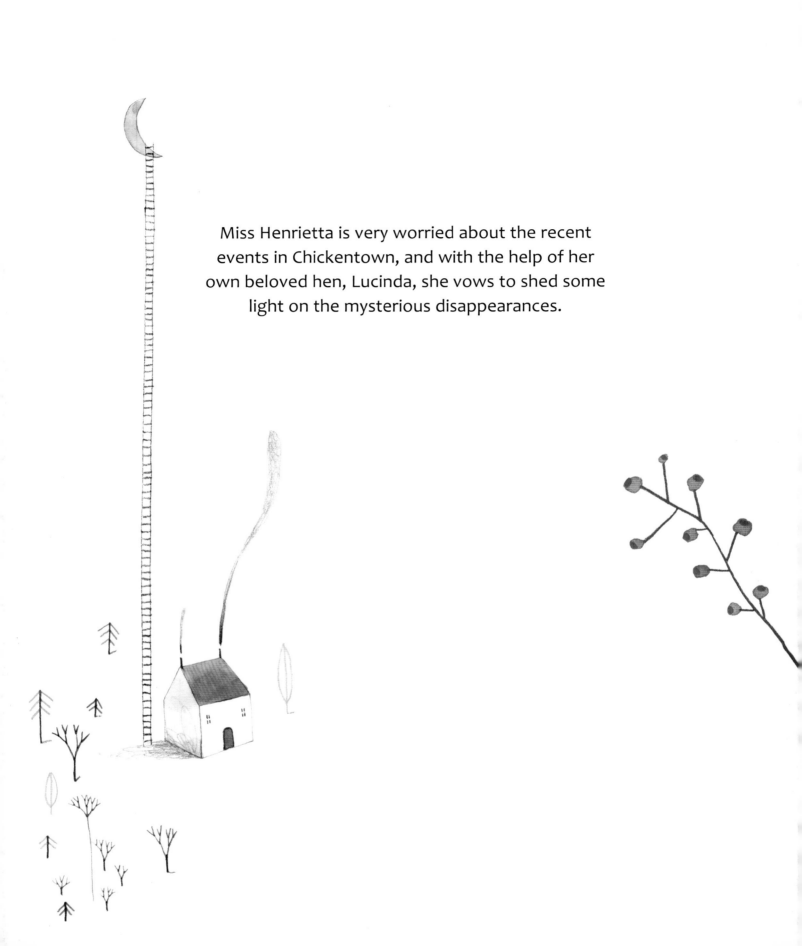

Miss Henrietta is very worried about the recent events in Chickentown, and with the help of her own beloved hen, Lucinda, she vows to shed some light on the mysterious disappearances.

Miss Henrietta has noticed that the attacks always occur at night, so she feeds Lucinda a magic star, luminous and bright.

And something extraordinary happens.

Anyone who tries to harm the wise witch's hen will be marked forever. They will shine, as Lucinda now does, with the glow of a thousand lights.

The plan Miss Henrietta has devised is as brilliant as it is dangerous.

Miss Henrietta and Lucinda embrace each other for courage.

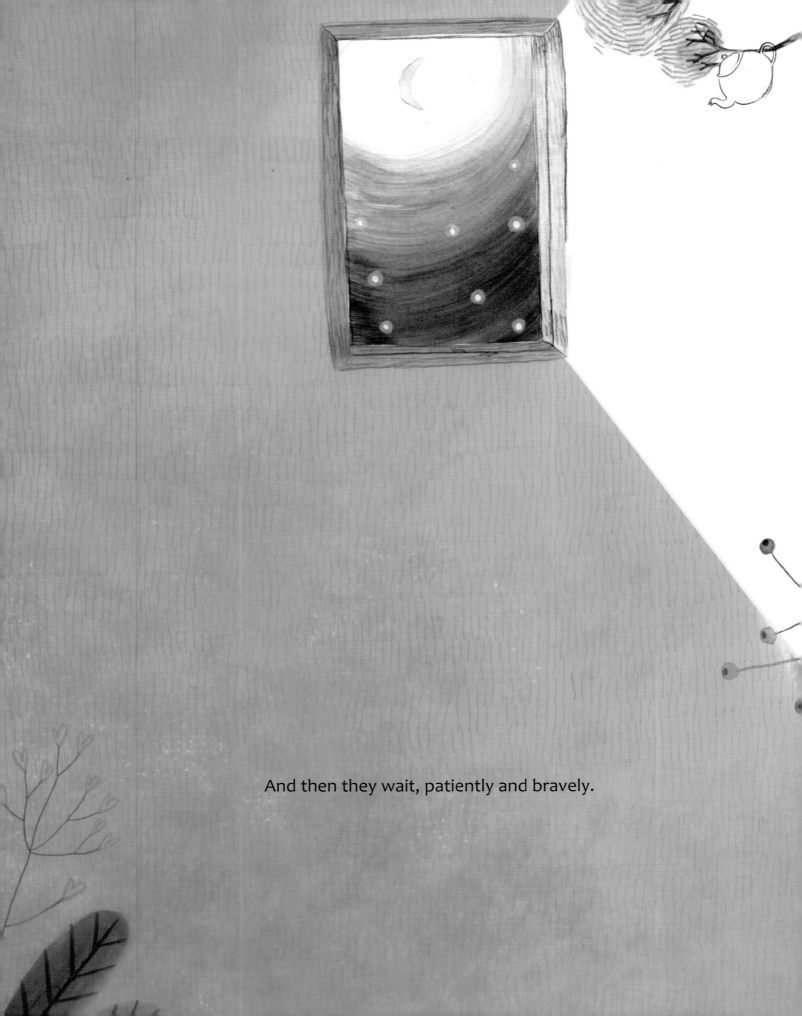

And then they wait, patiently and bravely.

A shadow suddenly appears
in Lucinda's room.
Who could it be?

Whoever they are, they can't possibly be
prepared for what comes next.

A fox! It's a fox!

Thanks to Miss Henrietta's spell, a trail
of light follows the escaping animal. She runs
as fast as she can after it.

Miss Henrietta comes to a sudden stop.
What is this little house doing in the middle of the forest?
The four missing hens are inside! Scarlett, Gwendolyn, Rufina,
and Clarabelle are all safe and sound.
But where is the fox?
There is no sign of him anywhere.

The next day, with all the hens safely home in Chickentown, the Golden Feather competition can finally proceed. For the first time ever, the jury is unanimous. Lucinda wins the trophy! She is indeed the bravest hen that ever was—as well as the only one in the world that glows in the dark.

Of course, the citizens of Chickentown never quite
understood why the fox kidnapped and hid
the chickens instead of devouring them.
Aren't hens a delicacy for foxes?

The answer to these questions is stranger than anyone—even a wise witch—will ever know.

©2021 CHOUETTE PUBLISHING (1987) INC.
Original title: El enigma de Villagallina by Albert Arrayás
First published in Spain by Babulinka Libros, Barcelona
©2017 Mar Moya and Albert Arrayás for the original idea
©2017 Albert Arrayás, for the illustrations
©2017 Marlet, Mar Moya and Albert Arrayás, for the text
"Rights negotiated through Ute Körner Literary Agent — www.uklitag.com"

CrackBoom! Books is an imprint of Chouette Publishing (1987) Inc.

Translation: Carine Laforest

Chouette Publishing would like to thank the Government of Canada and SODEC
for their financial support.

The illustration of this book was supported by a grant from the Institut Ramon Llull.

institut
ramon llull
Catalan Language and Culture

Bibliothèque et Archives nationales du Québec and Library and Archives Canada
cataloguing in publication

Title: The Chickentown mystery / Albert Arrayás; translation, Carine Laforest.
Other titles: Enigma de Villagallina. English
Names: Arrayás, Albert, 1990- author. | Laforest, Carine, translator.
Description: Translation of: El enigma de Villagallina.
Identifiers: Canadiana 20200095056 | ISBN 9782898022746 (hardcover)
Classification: LCC PZ7.1.A77 Ch 2021 | DDC j863/.7—dc23

Legal deposit – Bibliothèque et Archives nationales du Québec, 2021.
Legal deposit – Library and Archives Canada, 2021.

CRACKBOOM! BOOKS

©2021 Chouette Publishing (1987) Inc.
2515 De La Renaissance Avenue
Boisbriand, Quebec J7H 1T9 Canada
crackboombooks.com

Printed in Foshan, China
10 9 8 7 6 5 4 3 2 1 CHO2121 DEC2020

Albert Arrayás is a Spanish author and illustrator. He studied Fine Arts at the University of Barcelona. His beautiful and delicate illustrations have already been published in more than 25 children's books and he regularly collaborates with magazines and publishers in Spain.

The Chickentown Mystery is the second book he has written and illustrated. This story was inspired by Albert's own chickens, whom he describes as funny and sensitive creatures. He says that anyone who has shared their life with chickens will agree with him.

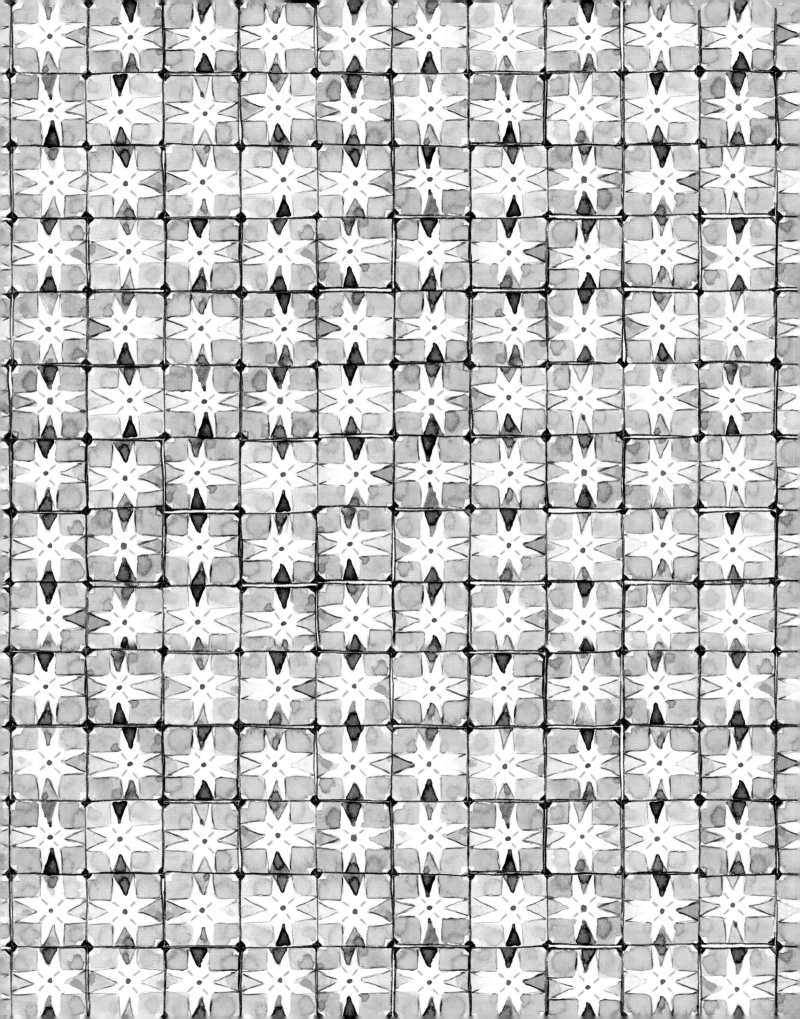